Sabby and the Dream Monsters

For Donald who did it
H.O.
To Jane and Darren
P.U.

ORCHARD BOOKS
96 Leonard Street, London EC2A 4XD
Orchard Books Australia
14 Mars Road, Lane Cove, NSW 2066
ISBN 1 86039 383 7 hardback
ISBN 1 84121 597 X paperback
First published in Great Britain in 1999
First paperback publication in 2000
Text © Hiawyn Oram 1999
Illustrations © Peter Utton 1999
The rights of Hiawyn Oram to be identified as the author and Peter Utton as the
illustrator of this work has been asserted by them in accordance with the Copyright,
Designs and Patents Act, 1988.
A CIP catalogue record for this book is available from the British Library.
1 2 3 4 5 6 7 8 9 10 hardback
1 2 3 4 5 6 7 8 9 10 paperback
Printed in Hong Kong / China

Sabby and the Dream Monsters

Hiawyn Oram ☆ Peter Utton

 ORCHARD BOOKS

Sabby was having a bad monster dream.

Sabby was having another
bad monster dream.

Sabby was having ANOTHER bad monster dream.

"Oh dear," sighed her
father. "You really are
a big bad monster-dream
dreamer, aren't you?"
"Yes," sniffed Sabby.

"Well, what are we going to do about it?" said her mother.

"I'll think of something," said her father. "In the morning."

In the morning, Sabby's father began thinking.
He scratched his chin and got out his notebook.

"Now tell me about these monsters,"
he said.

"Well," said Sabby. "There's the one
with the gleeky ears and the bloggy
eyes and the fat slodgy feet."

Her father's hair stood on end.

"Ah, ha," he said, writing
in his notebook. "The
GLEEKENBLOG
SLODGEFOOT
Monster. Go on."

Sabby got out her paints and started painting a picture.

"And there's this one," she said. "That's all bobbly and glumpy with big wiry wings."

"Yikes!" yelled her father scribbling furiously. "The BOBBLYGLUMP FLYER Monster. Go on."

"All right," said Sabby, running out of the room. "Wait here."

When she came back she was dressed like a monster. She looked so frightening, even her mother hid behind the sofa.

"Don't worry," said Sabby. "This is the WORST one. This is the really REALLY MUNGY Monster."

"Wow," said her father. "These are real *bad* bad monster-dream monsters."

"I told you," said Sabby. "NOW will you do something?"

"I'll try," sighed her father, picking up his notebook and disappearing into his workshop.

Sabby heard him lock the door.

She heard sawing. She heard drilling. She heard hammering. All day she heard sawing and drilling and hammering, the purr of a sewing machine and her father talking to himself...

"Gleekenblog...

Bobblyglump...

and Mungy One...

Just you wait..."

And then, at last, that evening, as she was putting on her pyjamas, she heard her father unlock the workshop door and come out. With him came a big cardboard box.

"Well?" said Sabby. "Is what's in there what you've thought of. Because if it isn't, I'm not going to bed again, ever!"

"Call your mother, jump under the covers, close your eyes and we'll see," said her father.

So Sabby called her mother,
jumped under the covers
and closed her eyes.

And when her father said open them
and she opened them, there beside
her on the pillow was...

"A PROPER MONSTER!" screamed Sabby's mother. "No, no, not a proper monster!" said Sabby's father. "It's a NO-MORE BAD-MONSTER-DREAM Monster. Sabby's very own No-More-Bad-Monster-Dream Monster to keep away her Monster Dream-Monsters."

Sabby sat up and took a closer look.

Then she curled up happily and drew the No-More-Bad-Monster-Dream Monster towards her.

"Of course!" she sighed. "That's just what he is and I think I'll call him Bliff. Good night!"

"Good night!" said her mother.

"Sleep tight!" said her father.

"I will," sighed Sabby.

"She will," added Bliff. "I'll see to that."

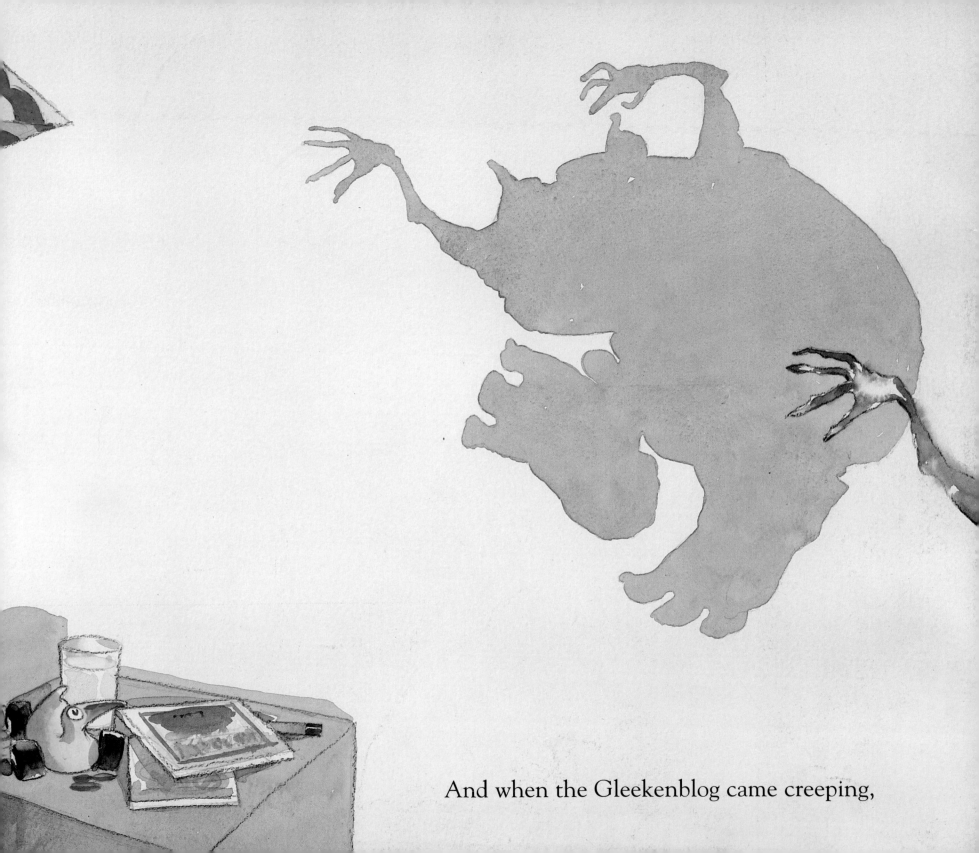

And when the Gleekenblog came creeping,

Bliff went BIFF, BLIFF and SCAT!

When Bobblyglump came creeping, Bliff went
SCAT! WATCH IT, MATEY! OFF!

When the Really Really Mungy One
came sliding and slurping, Bliff couldn't have
cared less. BLIFF! SCAT! OFF! OUT!
he went and...NEVER COME NEAR
SABBY'S DREAMS AGAIN!

And in the morning, when Sabby woke, she picked Bliff up and ran to tell her father the good news.

"It worked!" She kissed him. "Thank you! Thank you! Thank you! But you'd better get up and go to your workshop!"

"Why?" yawned her father.

"Because now there IS such a thing as a No-More-Bad-Monster-Dream Monster, every child in the world is going to want one, aren't they, Bliff?"

But Bliff didn't answer. He was snoring
his head off...which, after the night's work
he'd had, was hardly that surprising.